Animalium
COLOURING BOOK

Curated by KATIE SCOTT

BPP

Lions

Many of the best-known big cats, such as lions and cheetahs, live in open grasslands. They are carnivores with athletic bodies, and are famous for their stealth and speed. Cats have good eyesight even in dim light, their ears and sense of smell are sensitive, and their whiskers pick up sensory information to help them hunt at dusk. Second only to the tiger in size, the lion is immediately recognisable thanks to its mane. It lives in prides where the females hunt together for food.

Penguins

Penguins are instantly recognisable thanks to their upright stance and black and white plumage. Ungainly on land and completely flightless, penguins are fast and agile swimmers, with large webbed feet, and wings that have adapted to act like flippers in the water. They live across the Southern Hemisphere and most species have evolved to survive in cold environments. Their feathers, densely packed and waterproof, offer excellent insulation, and their blood flow has adapted so that they do not freeze when standing on ice.

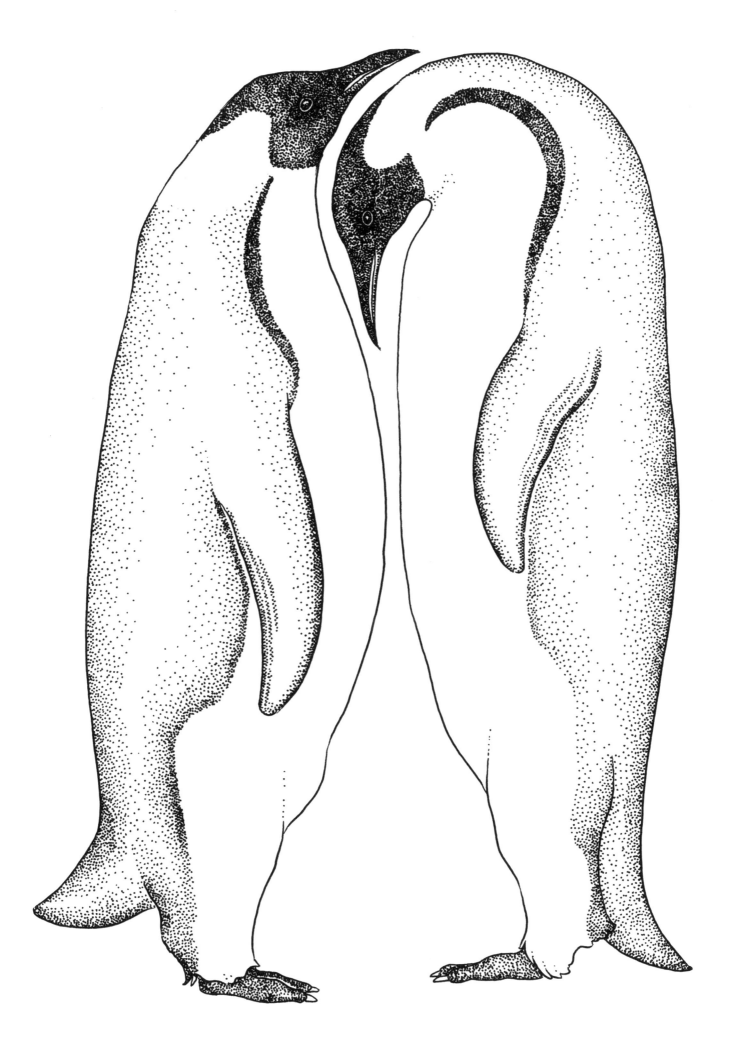

Habitat:
Coral Reefs

Coral reefs can be found in warm, clear, shallow parts of the ocean floor, and are colourful environments teeming with life. The reefs are hard, stony structures gradually formed over thousands of years by tiny animals called coral polyps. Over 4,000 species of fish can be found living in coral reefs. Their bright colouring helps them to camouflage themselves and confuse predators, and many keep to confined areas where they know every nook and cranny of the corals to hide in.

Hummingbirds and Birds-of-paradise

Hummingbirds are some of the smallest birds in the animal kingdom, measuring less than 13 centimetres long. However, they display a formidable dexterity and precision when flying, being the only birds able to fly backwards. Hummingbirds are also able to hover in one spot in order to extract nectar from flowers. They accomplish this by flapping their wings up to 80 times a second, which creates their distinctive 'hum'. The bird-of-paradise (centre) is famous for its elaborate ritual mating dance in which it displays its colourful plumes.

Moths

Moths are a type of insect, closely related to butterflies. They are mostly nocturnal and, unlike butterflies, they have feathery antennae. The atlas moth *(top)* is considered to have the largest wings of any insect, with a wingspan of nearly 30 centimetres. The luna moth *(bottom)* is known for its distinctive wing-shape – the moth mimics fallen leaves in order to avoid predators.

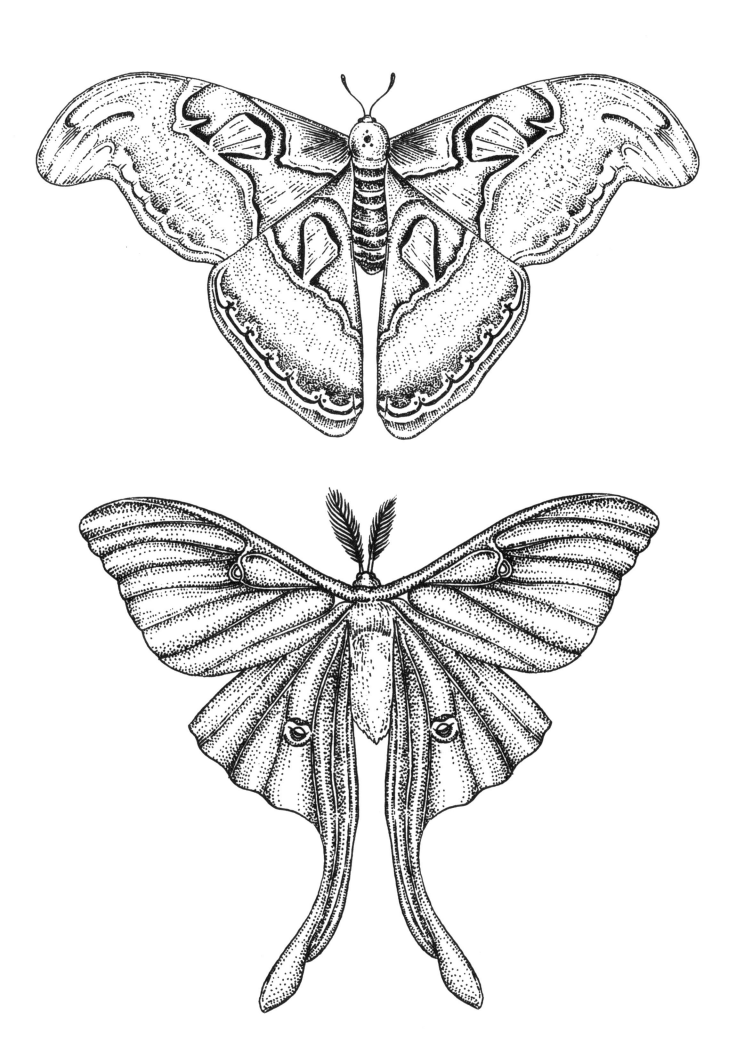

Fish

Fish are cold-blooded vertebrates (animals with jointed spines) and live in nearly all aquatic environments. With 32,000 species, there is a broader diversity of fish than any other type of vertebrate. There are four categories of fish: ancient jawless fish, such as lampreys *(bottom left)*; cartilaginous fish, such as sharks and rays *(see page 48)*; common ray-finned fish with bony skeletons, such as mullet *(top left)*, sockeye salmon *(top right)*, mackerel *(bottom centre)* and oarfish *(bottom right)*; and lobe-finned fish, such as coelacanth *(top centre)*.

Turtles and Tortoises

Turtles are members of an order of reptiles called Testudines, which also includes tortoises and aquatic terrapins. Turtles' shells are attached to their bodies, and so their protective armour can never be taken off or left behind. Land-dwelling tortoises have higher, domed shells, whilst aquatic species have flatter shells. To hide inside their shells, some species fold their head alongside their shoulder, whilst others retract their neck and head backwards. Box turtles have a hinged bony plate that allows their shells to close completely.

Monkeys

De Brazza's monkey *(top left)* is sociable and communicative, imparting information visually, vocally and via touch. Its robust feet allow it to roam the forest floor more successfully than other primates. The mantled guereza *(top right)* lives in groups and spends the majority of its time in trees, but can come down to the forest floor to feed. At night, a sentry keeps watch for predators. The golden lion tamarin *(bottom)* forms strong bonds with members of its group and is known to share its food and care for another's offspring.

Frogs

Frogs are a type of amphibian, from the Greek word *amphibios*, meaning 'living both in water and on land'. Most adult frogs have strong back legs that make them excellent at jumping and swimming, and some species have adapted to be able to climb and glide through the air. They develop good hearing and loud croaks, allowing them to communicate with one another across long distances. Their colouring can be mottled and subdued to camouflage them, or bright and colourful to ward predators off.

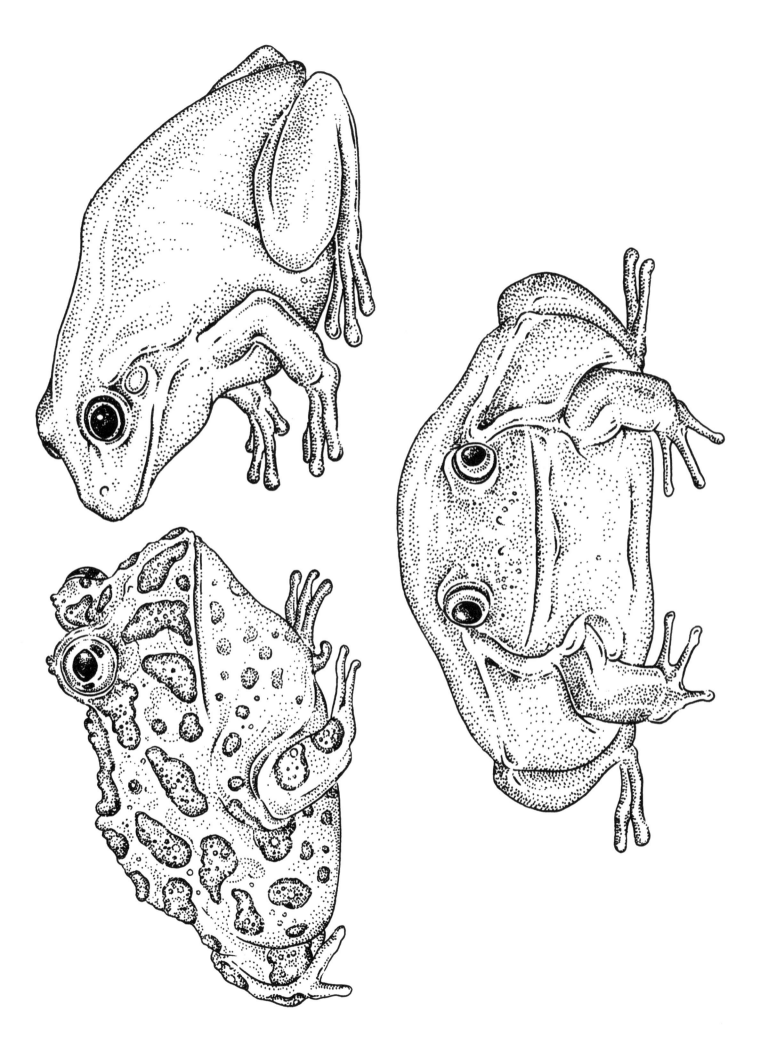

Octopuses

Octopuses have large brains and advanced senses, making them intelligent and sociable creatures. They have sucker-like tentacles, and swim by taking in water and shooting it out to move forward by jet propulsion. Octopuses can change the colour and pattern of their bodies to camouflage themselves or ward off predators. They also produce ink and, when threatened, can release an inky cloud to confuse predators.

Birds of Prey

Birds of prey are formidable hunters. Many have no predators of their own. They have acute senses, sharp beaks for tearing apart flesh, and strong feet that usually feature long talons with an opposable hind claw for snatching their target. Birds of prey are typically fast and agile flyers, though some, such as vultures, are scavengers, and eat the flesh of animals that are already dead, called carrion, rather than hunting live prey.

Snakes

There are around 3,400 species of snake, and they can be found on every continent except Antarctica. All are carnivorous and possess large, flexible jaws, which allow them to eat prey much larger than their own heads. Because their teeth are designed for killing, but not chewing, they swallow their victims whole. Different species have their own methods of attack; around one in ten species has a venomous bite, whilst others use constriction – crushing prey to death by coiling their bodies around their victims.

Giraffes

The African Masai giraffe is the tallest land mammal on Earth. Its long legs and neck have evolved to allow it to feed from the treetops, and its long and flexible tongue extends to gather in twigs and leaves. Like most other grazing herbivores, it has wide, flat teeth suited to grinding down vegetation. When competing for a mate, male giraffes duel by battering one another with their long necks.

Flightless Birds

The common ostrich *(bottom)* is the largest and fastest-running bird on Earth. This flightless bird can reach speeds of up to 70 kilometres per hour thanks to its powerful long legs, which can stride up to 4.9 metres. Ostriches have been known to kill lions with their kick! The cassowary *(top)* is recognisable thanks to its hornlike casque and two red wattles that hang from its throat. It has a dagger-like claw on its inner toe, with which it defends itself, charging down and spearing its target.

Seals and Walruses

Seals and walruses are semi-aquatic carnivorous mammals. Although they spend much of their life in water, they breathe air and breed on land. The Weddell seal *(top)* is a relatively large and common species of seal, typically found around the South Pole. When it is hunting, it can stay underwater for up to 80 minutes. The walrus *(bottom)* has prominent tusks, which can grow up to one metre long. It uses these tusks to compete for a mate, and to dig holes in the ice.

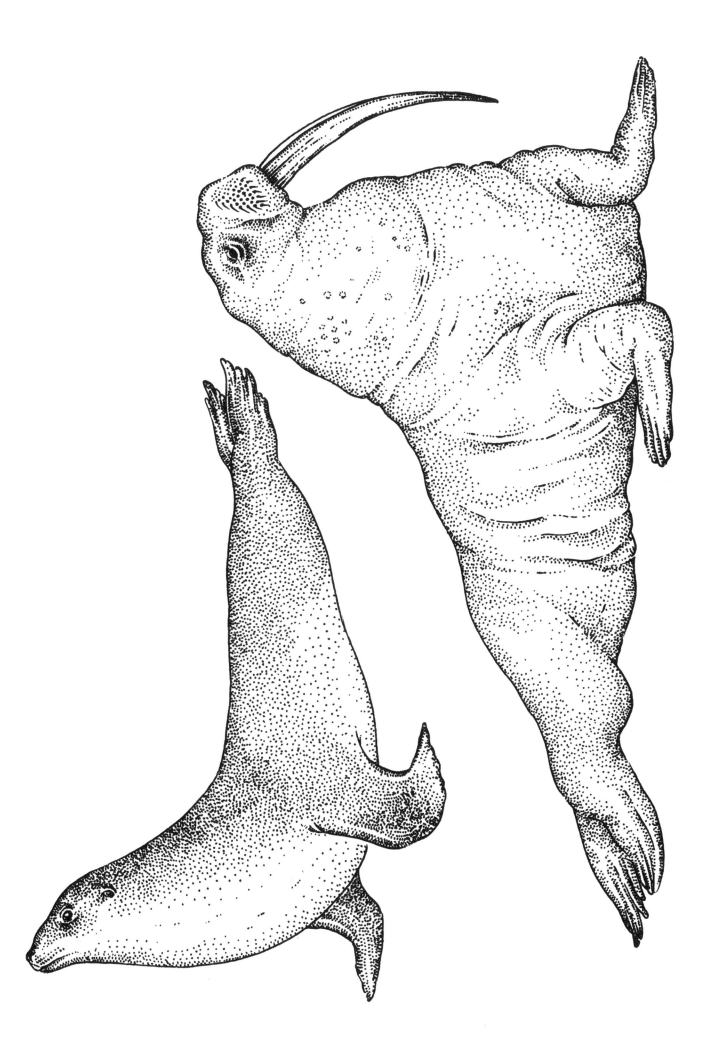

Habitat: Woodlands

Woodland habitats are made up of trees, shrubs and grasses; the greater the variety of plants growing, the more animals it can support as a habitat. Many species of bird live in woodlands for some – or all – of the year. Some of the world's best-known songbirds can be found in this habitat, and although they can be difficult to spot, you can tell them apart by their complex and unique songs. Birds sing for lots of reasons: to assert their territory, attract a mate or alert others to danger.

Jellyfish

Jellyfish are carnivorous, and kill and eat other animals in order to survive. Because they are not built to chase or hunt down their victims, they are known as 'passive predators' that wait for other creatures to blunder into them. When unwitting prey brushes past a jellyfish's tentacles, a hairlike trigger is activated, causing a toxic capsule to eject from its body and harpoon its victim. A jellyfish sting can paralyse and kill its prey, and an unlucky encounter can be extremely painful – and sometimes fatal – for humans, too.

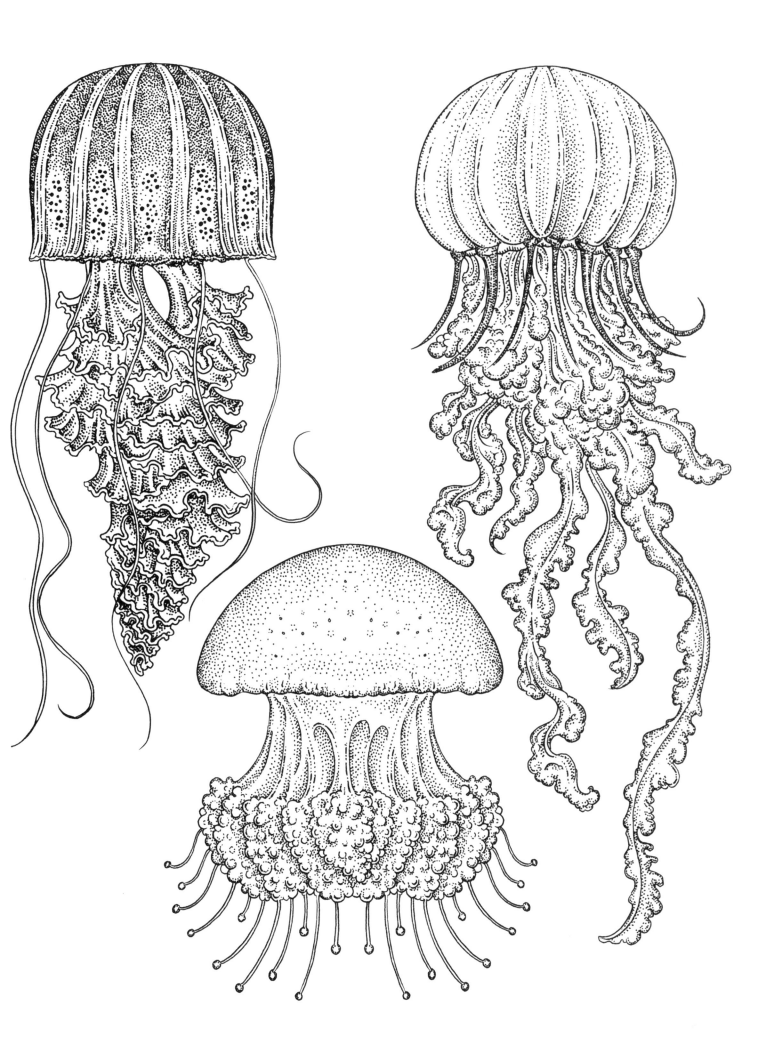

Sponges

Living exclusively underwater, sponges can be found in all habitats, from tropical seas to icy waters. With no nervous system or organs, they are incapable of thought or movement, and it would be easy to mistake them for plants. However, sponges are in fact animals that feed on bacteria, and sense and react to their environments. They have structures based around a hollow central cavity surrounded by small holes. This allows water to flow through the sponge's cavity, nourishing it with food and oxygen and carrying away carbon dioxide.

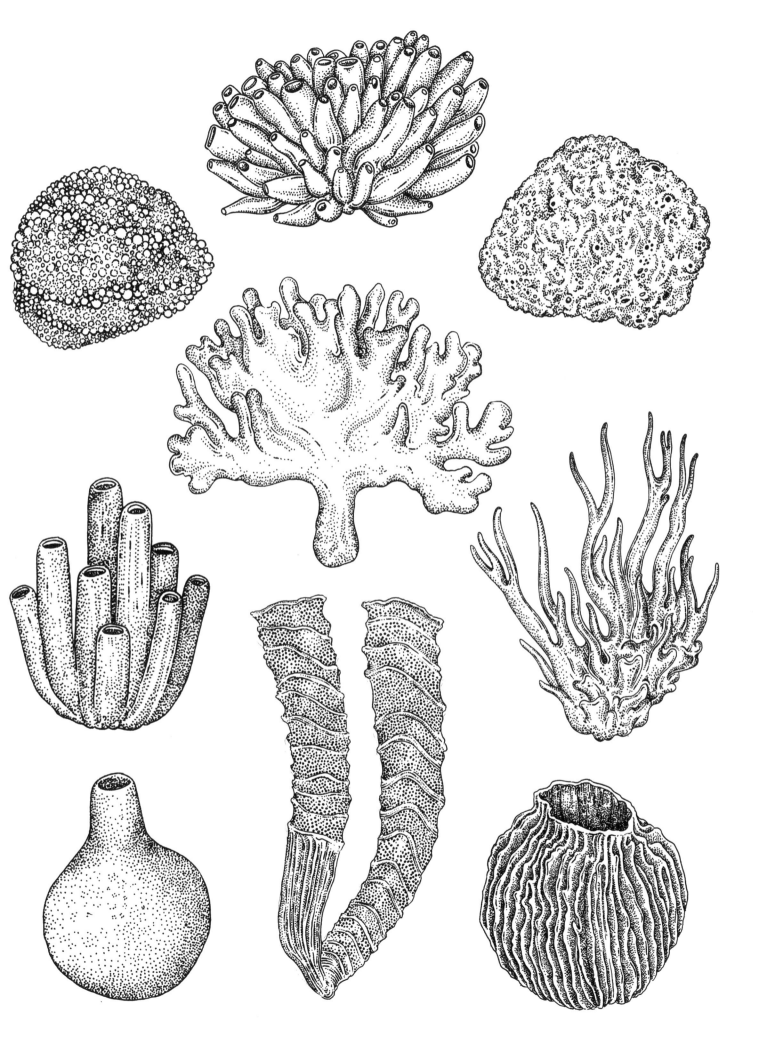

Narwhals

The narwhal is a medium-sized Arctic whale, reaching lengths of around 4.5 metres. It is most famous for its long, spiralled tusk – this can be up to 2.7 metres long, though its purpose is still unknown to us. The narwhal's specialised diet of Arctic sealife makes it especially vulnerable to the North Pole's changing climate.

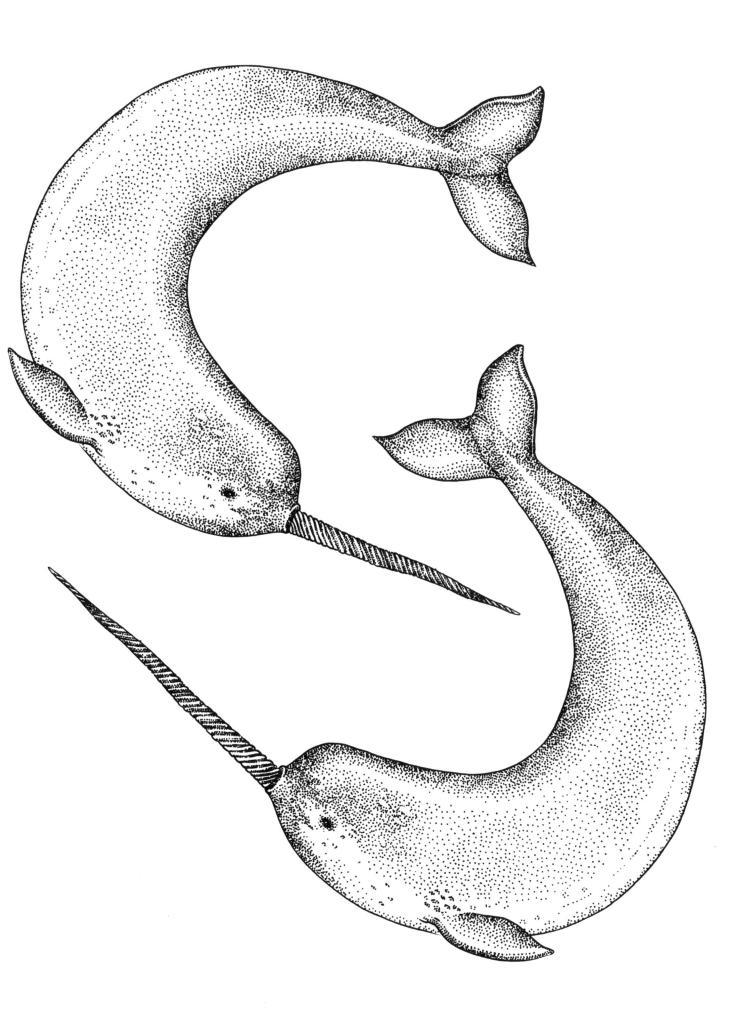

Parrots

Birds in tropical and exotic environments often display bright and colourful plumage. They are also social creatures, and many parrots form pairs that share a strong bond. The rosy-faced lovebird *(top)* is a green and yellow parrot that can often be spotted sleeping with its face turned towards its neighbour. The galah *(bottom left)* is pink in colour and is one of the most common cockatoos in Australia. The mallee ringneck parrot *(bottom right)* is a blue-green species, and the smallest of the Australian ringneck parrots.

Dragonflies, Mayflies and Crane flies

The emperor dragonfly *(bottom)* is the largest species of dragonfly on Earth, growing up to 7.8 centimetres long. It is a ferocious predator and rarely ever lands, even eating in flight. The pale snaketail dragonfly *(centre)* is smaller at 5 centimetres. It is rarely seen on cool days, preferring warmer temperatures. Mayflies *(top left)* have very short lives, and spend just one hour as adults before they die. Crane flies *(top right)* are nocturnal insects with long, delicate legs that are easily detachable.

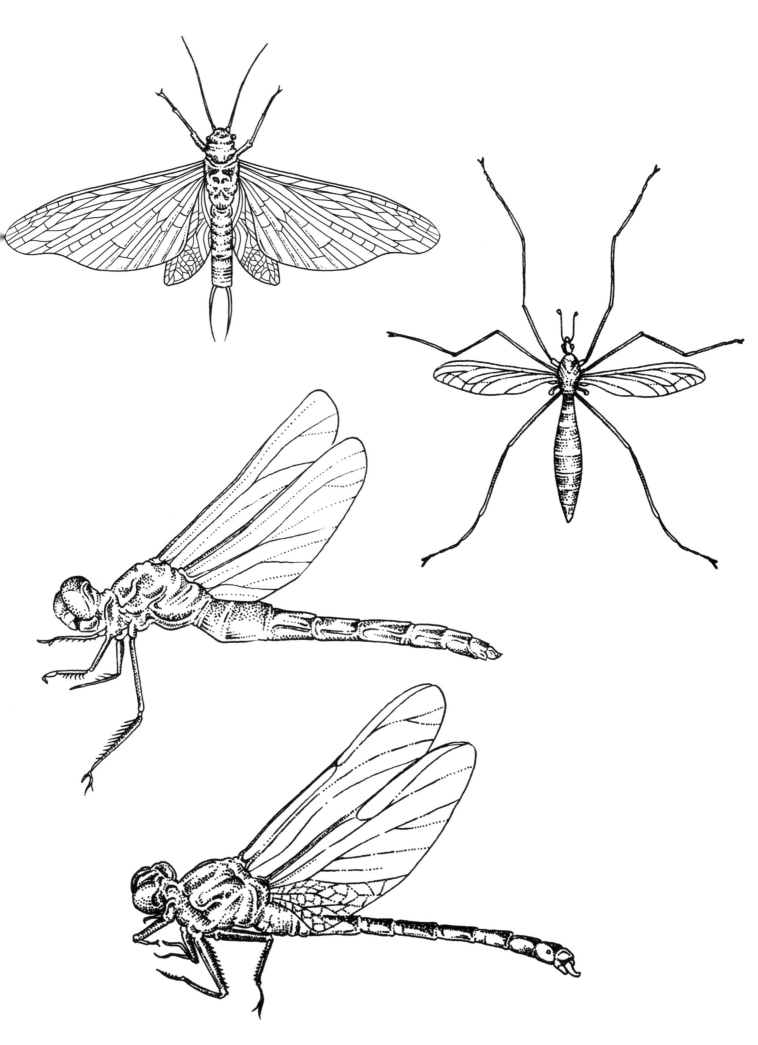

Marsupials

Marsupials give birth to their young at an earlier developmental stage than other mammals and carry them in the mother's protective pouch. The red kangaroo *(top)* is the largest species of marsupial. It is robustly built, with a tail strong enough to support its entire weight. To avoid overheating in the hot Australian sun, it licks its wrists. The koala *(bottom)* spends most of its life in the trees, out of danger from predators. Its diet of eucalyptus leaves is so poor in nutrients that a koala spends much of its day conserving energy by sleeping.

Grasshoppers and Wasps

The characteristic noise made by the common green grasshopper *(bottom)* is the sound of the male rubbing its hind legs together to attract a female mate. The plains lubber grasshopper *(centre)* is a much larger species, growing up to 5 centimetres long, and can jump over one metre! The common wasp *(top right)* is an aggressive species. When attacked it will send out an alarm for others to come and help. The great black wasp *(top left)* paralyses its prey with its sting, then carries it to an underground nest to feed its young.

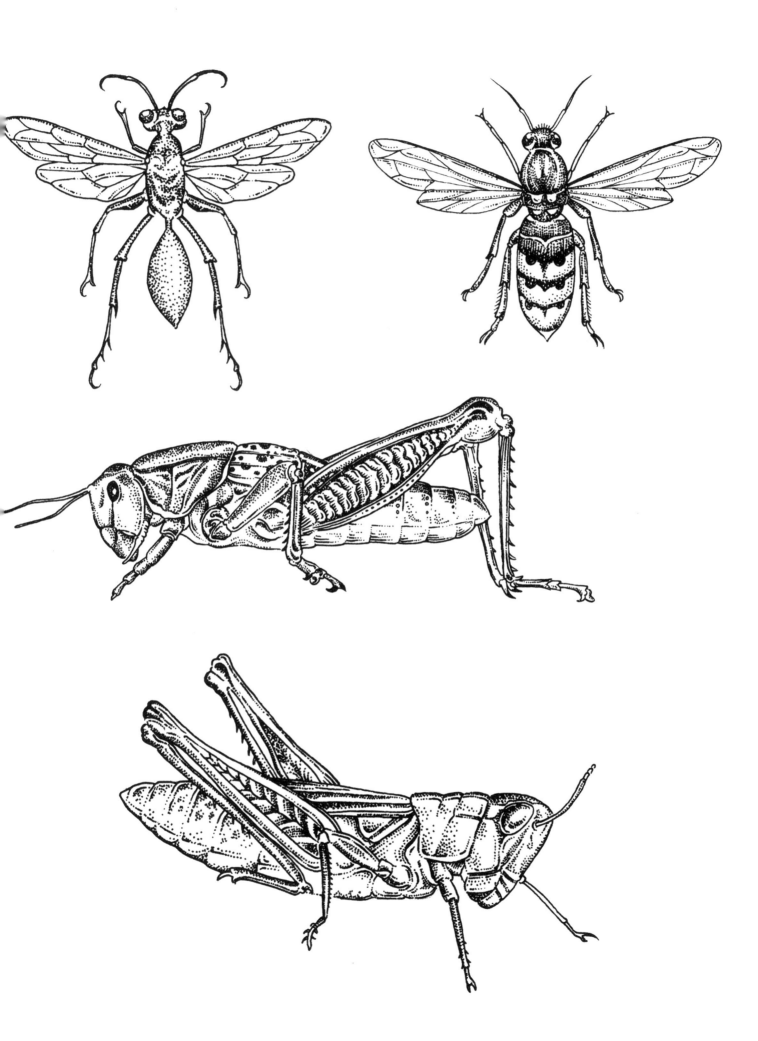

Rays

Rays have long, thin tails which are often armed with a venomous sting, wide disclike bodies, and 'wings' that they use to swim by flapping them like a flying bird. Some species are commonly seen leaping out of the water. While hidden under the sand, rays cannot use their eyes to see their prey. Instead, they use their sense of smell and electroreception to locate and hunt other fish.

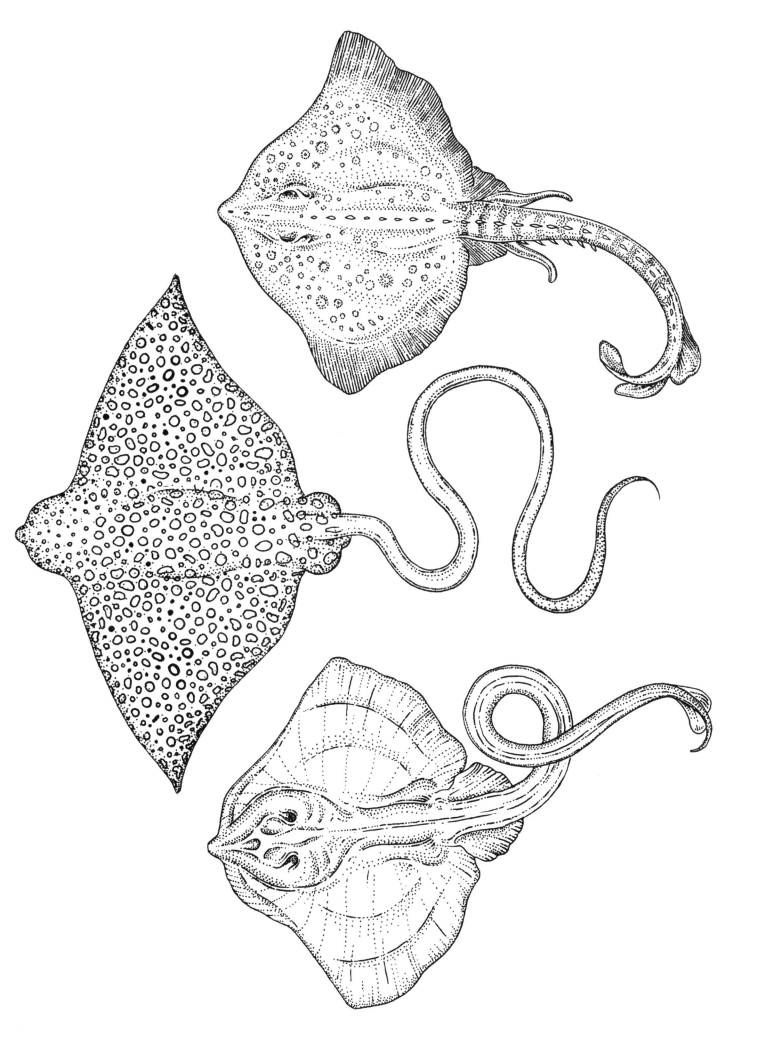

Salamanders

Like other amphibians, salamanders have smooth, moist skin, through which they absorb oxygen. Some salamanders like the Mandarin salamander *(left)* are brightly coloured, which warns predators that they are toxic and dangerous to eat. The Allen's worm salamander *(right)* is so called because of its long, thin body. It has no lungs at all, breathing entirely through its skin! Another notable feature of salamanders is their amazing ability to regenerate (regrow) a lost limb!

Whales

Despite spending the majority of their lives underwater, whales need to breathe air into their lungs. As a result, they have become excellent at holding their breath. Whales and dolphins take air in and expel carbon dioxide out through a blowhole located at the top of their heads. The humpback whale *(right)* is often seen breaching the water and slapping its tail. It communicates with other whales through its loud and complex song.

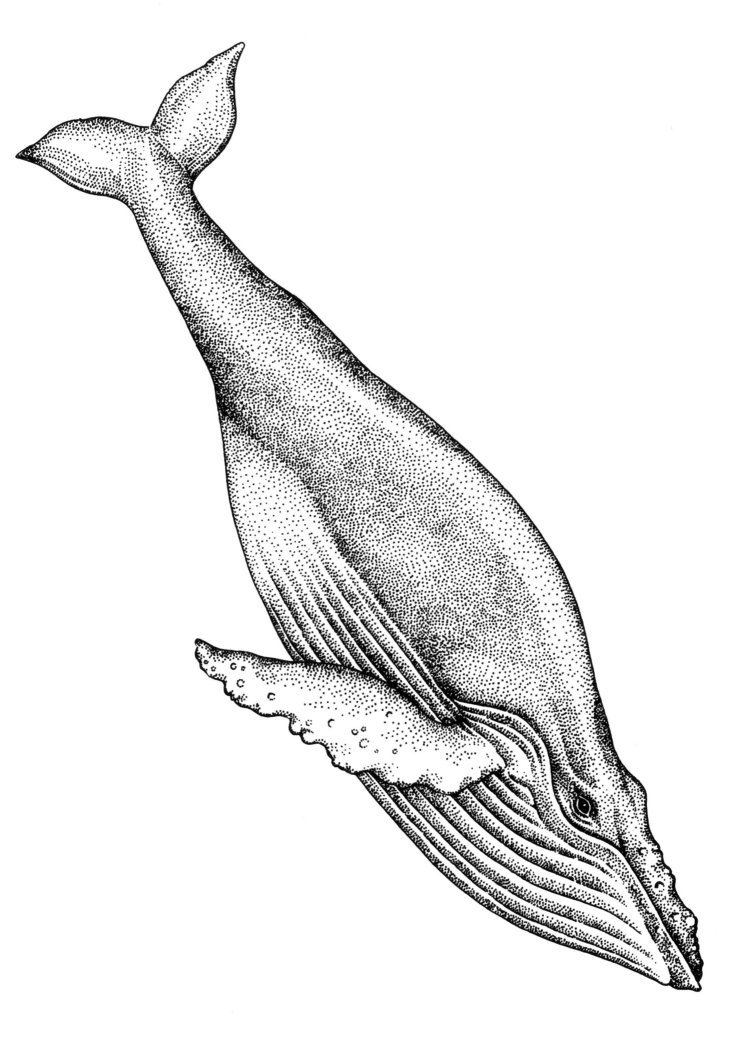

Toucans and Parakeets

Toucans *(top)* are known for their large and colourful bills. These bills are far from solely decorative, however. They use them to reach many fruits in a tree without needing to fly to a different branch. Their bills also help them to regulate their body temperature. Parakeets are a type of parrot. The rose-ringed parakeet *(bottom)* is blue in colour and found in West Africa, South-East Asia and areas in Europe.

Habitat: Coastal Waters

Coastal habitats appear where the sea meets the land. There are about 356,000 kilometres of coastline around the world, and the conditions there vary depending on the local climate, landscape and turbulence of the ocean. Coastal habitats are in constant flux as waves, tides and currents drag bodies of water across the shores, meaning there is continuous change to the landscape. However, rivers flooding into the sea and the waves' erosion of the land provide a constant source of rich nutrients, so life in coastal areas is the most abundant in the world.

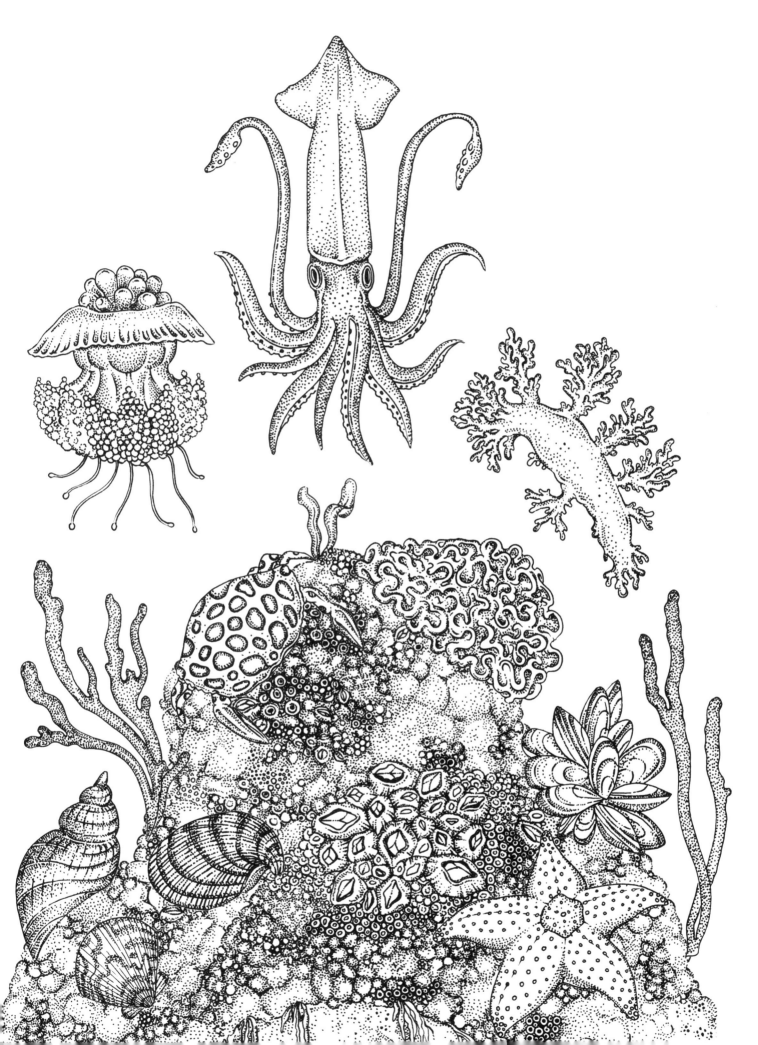

Dolphins

The short-beaked common dolphin is an intelligent and sociable creature. It grows up to 1.8 metres long and lives in groups of hundreds, if not thousands, of individuals. This species is well known for its aerial acrobatics. Like other water-based mammals, it locates its prey by using echolocation.

Tortoises

The Indian star tortoise *(top)* has a high tolerance of water, and so can be found in places that experience monsoon seasons. Its dome shape allows it to easily self-right. The leopard tortoise *(bottom)* is a large tortoise found in savannah habitats in Africa, where it can live for up to 100 years. It reaches lengths of around 50 centimetres. This tortoise's grasping toenails make it an agile walker, strong swimmer and surprisingly good climber.

Newts

The Alpine newt lives in forested and mountainous terrains throughout central Europe, near to freshwater streams and ponds. It hibernates during the cold winter months and emerges in the spring, when it feeds at night. The male, shown here, develops a crest to signal to females that he is ready to mate. It also changes colour from a camouflaging brown pattern to an eye-catching blue and orange. At the end of the mating season, the crest is re-absorbed into the body.

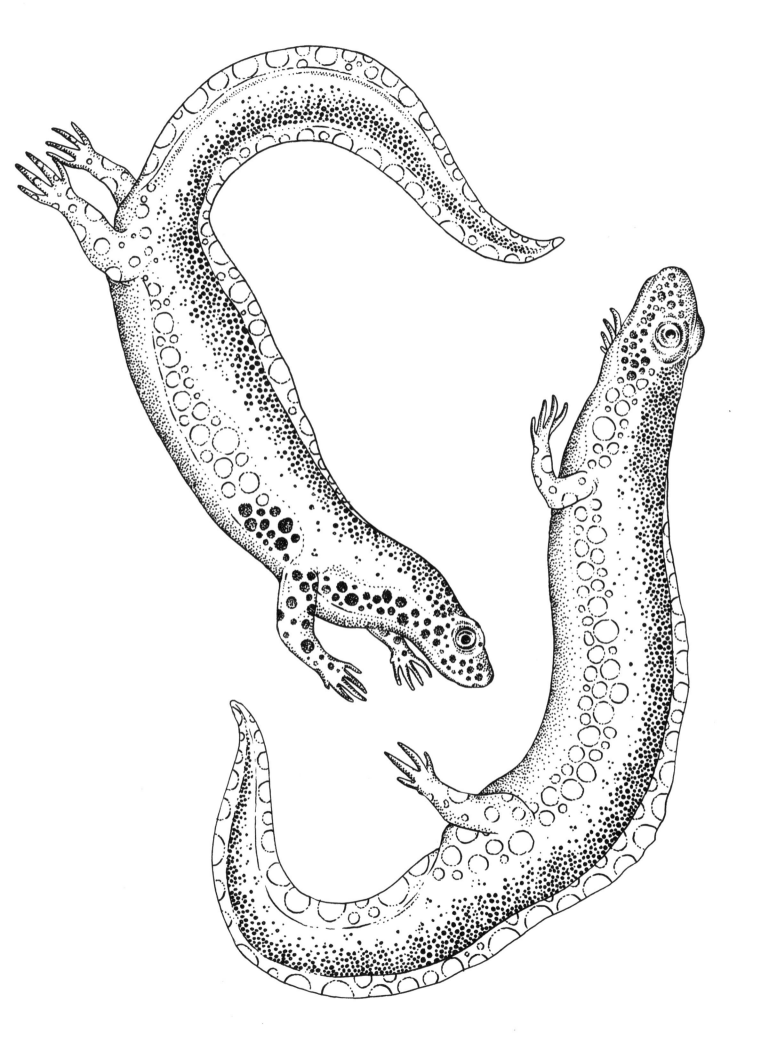

Rodents

Counting rats, mice, squirrels, hamsters, porcupines and beavers amongst their ranks, rodents make up around 40 per cent of all mammal species. All rodents have sharp front teeth that never stop growing, which means that they need to frequently gnaw on things to stop them from growing too long.

Owls

The spectacled owl *(top left)* is named for its dramatic white eyebrows which frame its eyes, resembling a pair of glasses. It is most vocal under the cover of darkness and makes a distinctive knocking or tapping sound. The southern white-faced owl *(bottom right)* has been nicknamed the 'transformer owl' thanks to the displays it puts on when threatened. If approached by an opponent slightly bigger than itself, it puffs up its feathers, attempting to seem larger. But when faced with a much greater predator, it flattens its feathers into its body, hides behind its wing and squints its eyes, to camouflage itself against a tree.

Bats

Bats are the only mammals that can fly. They are mostly nocturnal creatures, sleeping through the day, and hunting at twilight. Bats can detect prey and navigate in complete darkness thanks to echolocation. They build a detailed image of their surroundings by sending out high-pitched sound pulses and deducing from the time that noise takes to echo back what is located nearby.

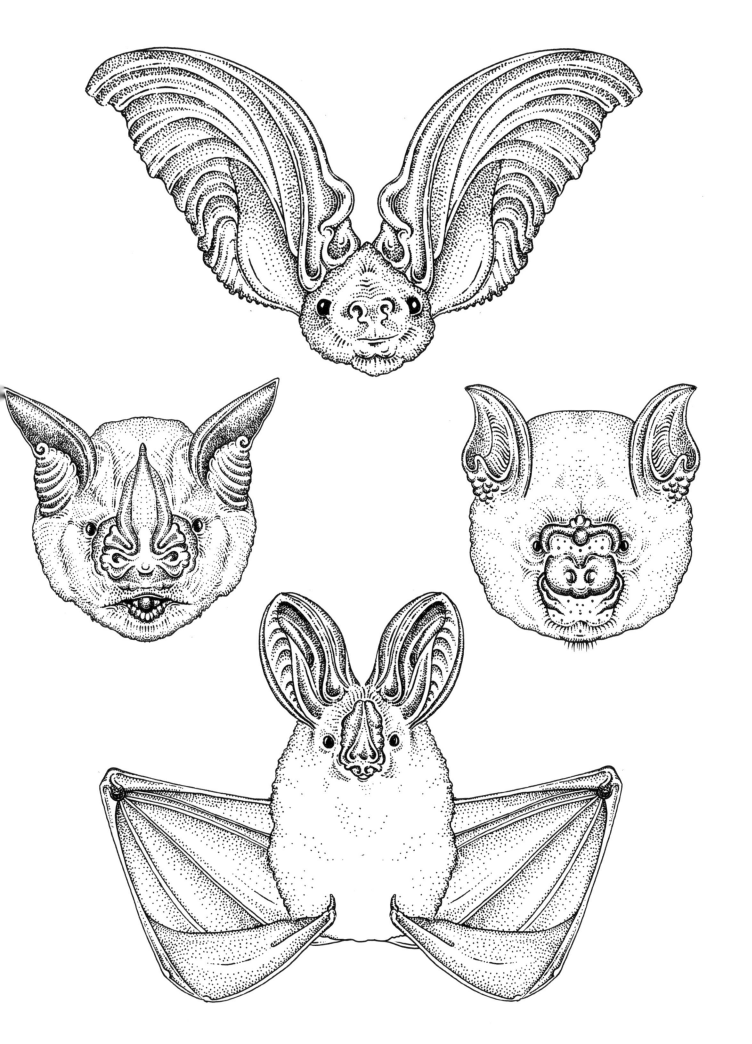

Gila Monsters

The Gila monster, a species of venomous lizard which lives in North America, spends much of its time underground. It feeds mostly on eggs and small creatures found in nests, and only eats between five and ten times a year – but when it does, it devours up to one third of its body mass. Unlike venomous snakes, which have hollow fangs, Gila monsters have very large, grooved teeth in their lower jaw. As they bite into their prey, poison travels down the grooves.

Primates

The playful mandrill *(right)* is one of the largest species of monkey in the world, and lives in the tropical rainforests of Africa. It spends its days foraging on the forest floor, returning to the trees to sleep. The highly intelligent chimpanzee *(left)* is one of humankind's closest relatives, and shares 98 per cent of our genes. It lives in groups of up to 150 individuals, in forested regions of Gabon, Cameroon and the Democratic Republic of the Congo.

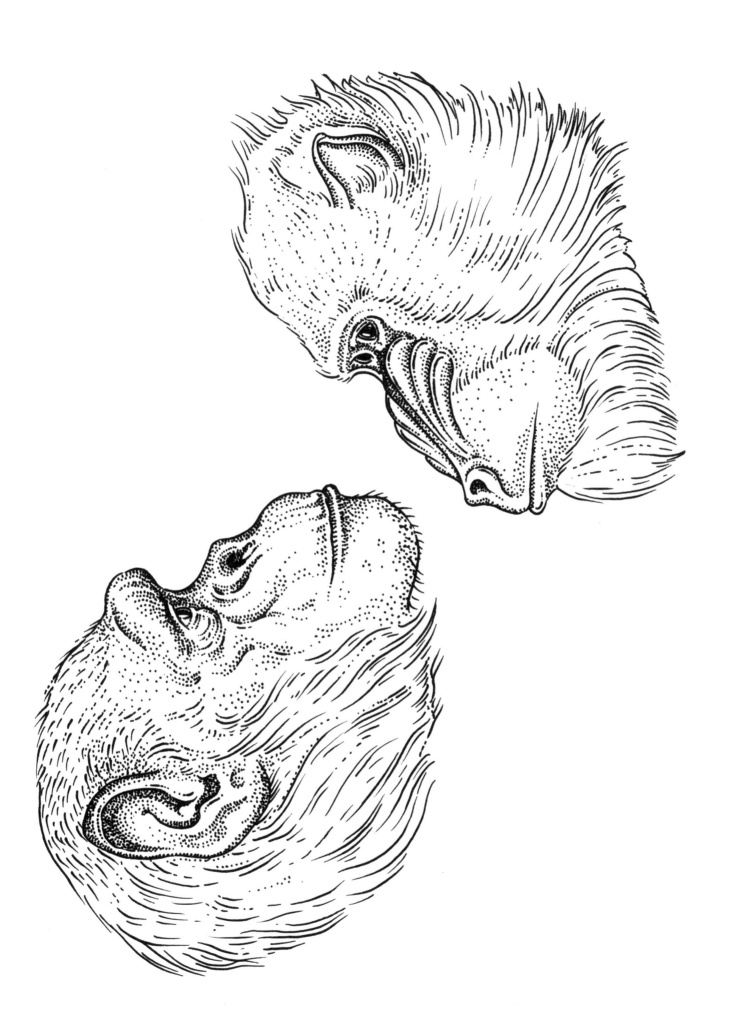

Habitat: Rainforests

Tropical rainforests are hot, humid areas, densely populated with trees and plants thanks to high levels of rainfall year-round. Amphibians are particularly well suited to this habitat: there are more than one thousand different species of frog in the Amazon Basin alone. The frequent rains create a warm, swampy environment that allows amphibians' skin to stay moist without having to stay close to ponds or rivers. As a result, many frogs are able to live in trees and lay their eggs in leaves, safely out of reach of predators.

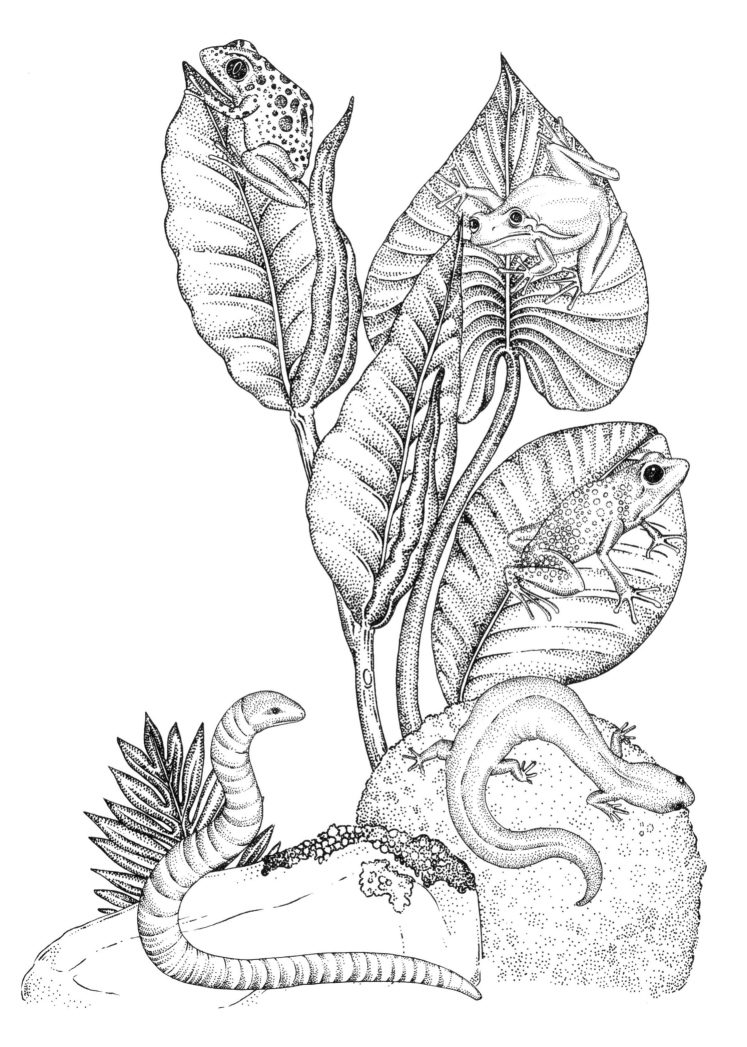

Wading Birds

Flamingos *(top)* are highly sociable creatures and live together in enormous flocks. Their colouring derives from a type of bacteria they ingest when eating their diet of shrimp. Consequently, flamingos range in colour from off-white to shocking coral pink. Herons *(bottom left)* are related to flamingos and are excellent fishermen. They use their S-shaped neck and sharp bill to spear fish with impressive speed. Grey-crowned cranes *(bottom right)* have a spectacular head crest, and perform elaborate courtship dances to attract a mate.

Elephants

Elephants are instantly recognisable thanks to their unique and flexible trunks, which they use to grab and hold objects with, their long, sharp tusks, and their large, flat ears. If an elephant begins to overheat, blood travels to its ears. They flap their ears in the breeze to cool the blood, which then circulates back through the body, keeping the elephant's temperature down. Elephants are the largest animals living on land. To help support their massive bulk, their legs are positioned straight underneath their bodies.

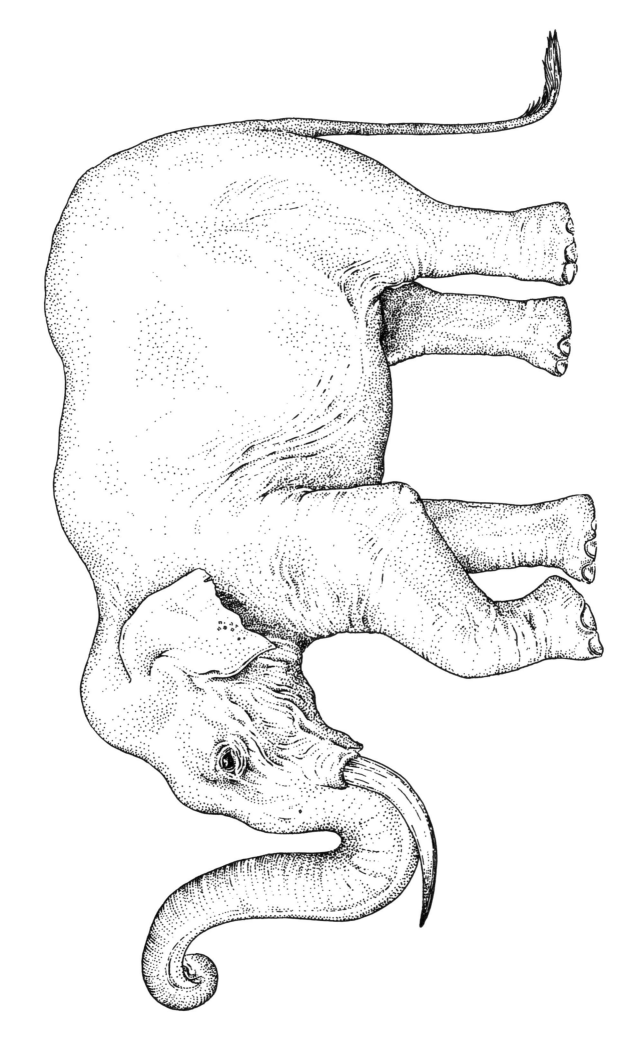

Barn Owls

The barn owl is the most common of all species of owl, and can be found on every continent except for Antarctica. Its name comes from its tendency to nest in man-made buildings, and it can be found living in both urban and rural environments. It has excellent night vision and directional hearing which allows it to detect creatures hidden from sight underground or beneath snow – a useful ability that allows it to hunt in deepest winter.

Habitat: Deserts

Deserts are areas defined by an extremely dry climate, where very little rain falls and few plants are able to grow. Some deserts are cold, but the largest deserts in the world are in areas where it is extremely hot, such as the Sahara Desert in Africa. Even in deserts that experience scorching heat by day, temperatures can plummet at night. Reptiles are especially suited to living in these environments because they are able to survive with little water. They take shelter beneath a rock during the hottest parts of the day and emerge to hunt in the evening.

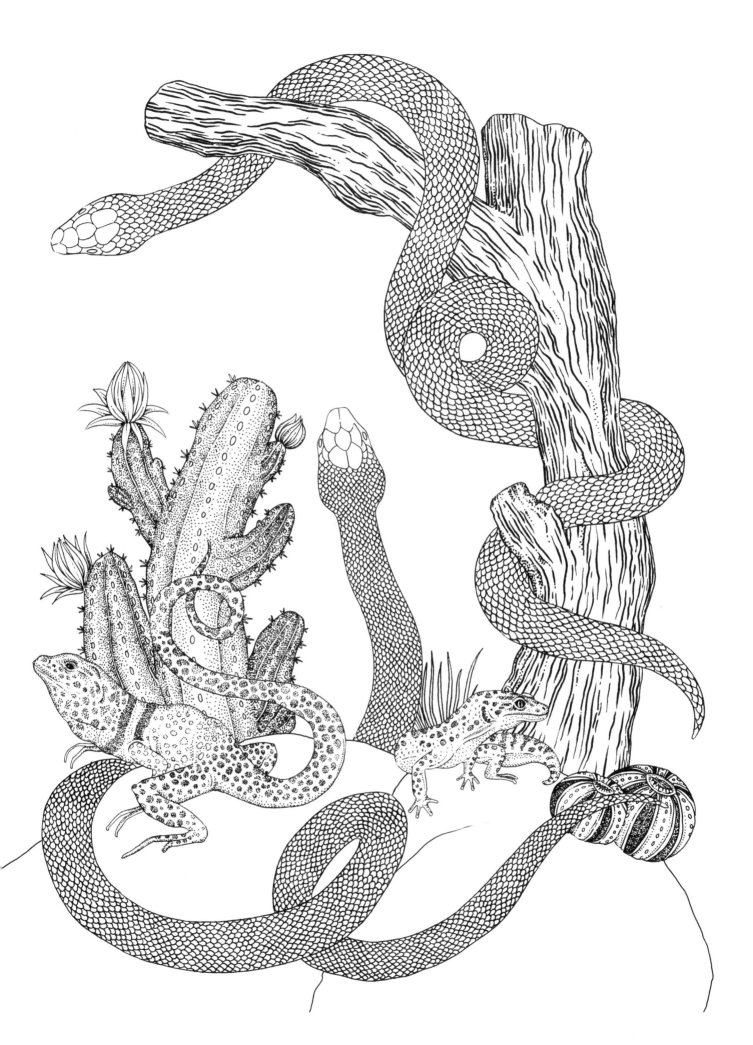

Tadpole to Frog

Frogs hatch from batches of eggs laid in water and spend their first days as aquatic larvae called tadpoles. Tadpoles have tails and gills that allow them to breathe underwater, and have a vegetarian diet. Soon after hatching, a tadpole starts to grow lungs, four legs and a large jaw, and its gills and tail disappear gradually. Its eyes, tongue and legs grow bigger and – sometimes in the space of only a day – the tadpole is transformed into an insect-eating frog. This entire transformation is known as metamorphosis.

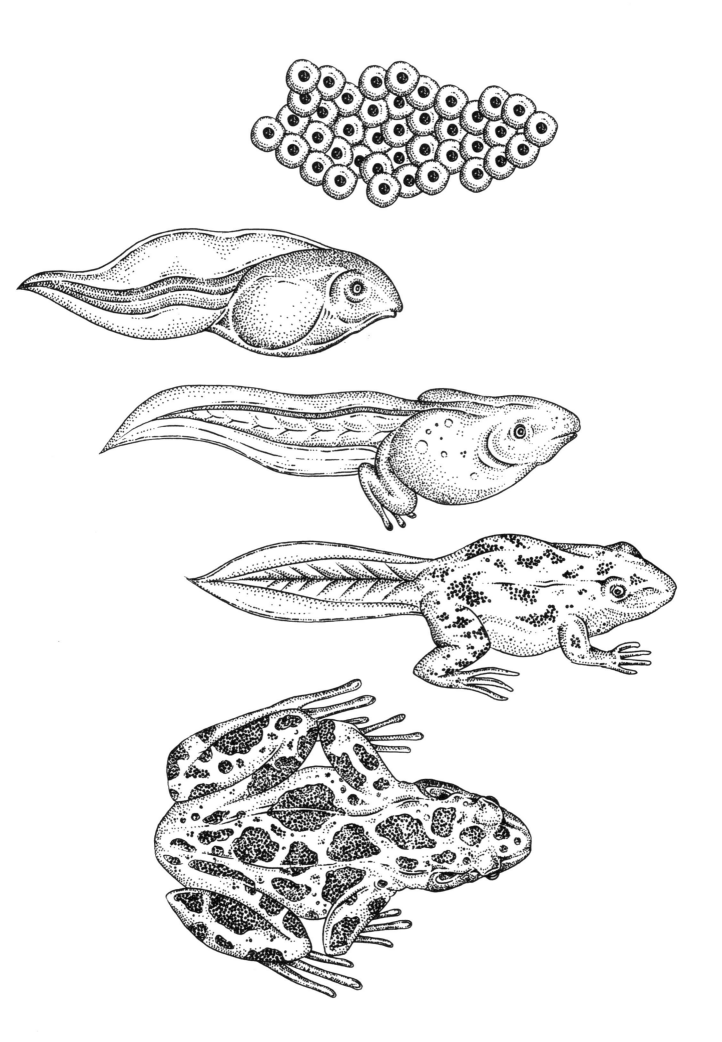

Rays and Skates

The heart-shaped smooth skate *(top)* is a relatively small species, so named because, unlike other skates, its shoulders and upper pelvic fins are not covered with rough denticles. It can be found in the waters of the north-west Atlantic. The shovelnose guitarfish *(bottom)* has an unusual shaped dorsal fin, which initially led people to believe it was a shark – it is in fact a species of ray. By day it lies on the ocean bed covered in sand, waiting to ambush a passing victim, and by night it cruises the seabed searching for prey.

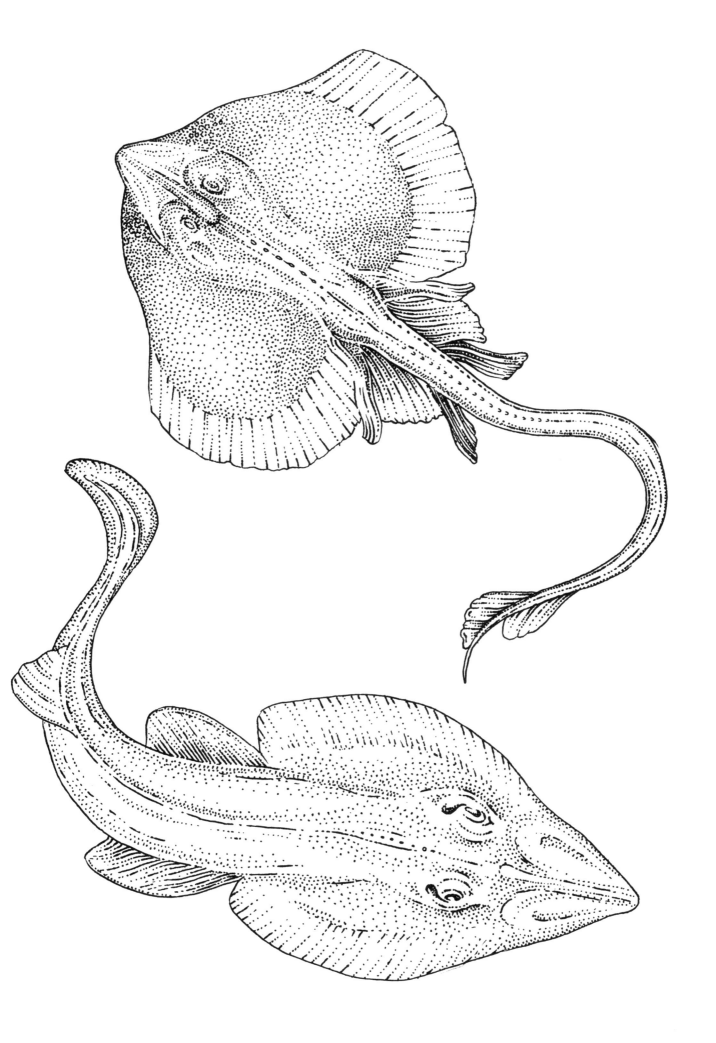

Habitat: Arctic Tundra

Around the North Pole is a cold, barren area called the tundra. This habitat is one of the most difficult places to survive on Earth due to its freezing temperatures, high winds, lack of shelter and scarcity of food and water. The ground is permanently frozen, which means there is little vegetation for animals to feed on. Cold-blooded reptiles and amphibians are not suited to this environment, but mammals can survive because they are warm-blooded and have furry coats that keep them from freezing.

Cnidaria

There are over 10,000 known cnidarian species and they come in widely diverse forms. Some, such as sea anemones and corals are static polyps, which means they attach themselves to rocks. Others, such as the box jellyfish, are free-moving, and contract their body shape to move. The stalked jellyfish *(top left)* is unlike other jellyfish because it spends its entire life attached to rocks or algae. The dahlia sea anemone *(bottom left)* has up to 160 short tentacles around its mouth.

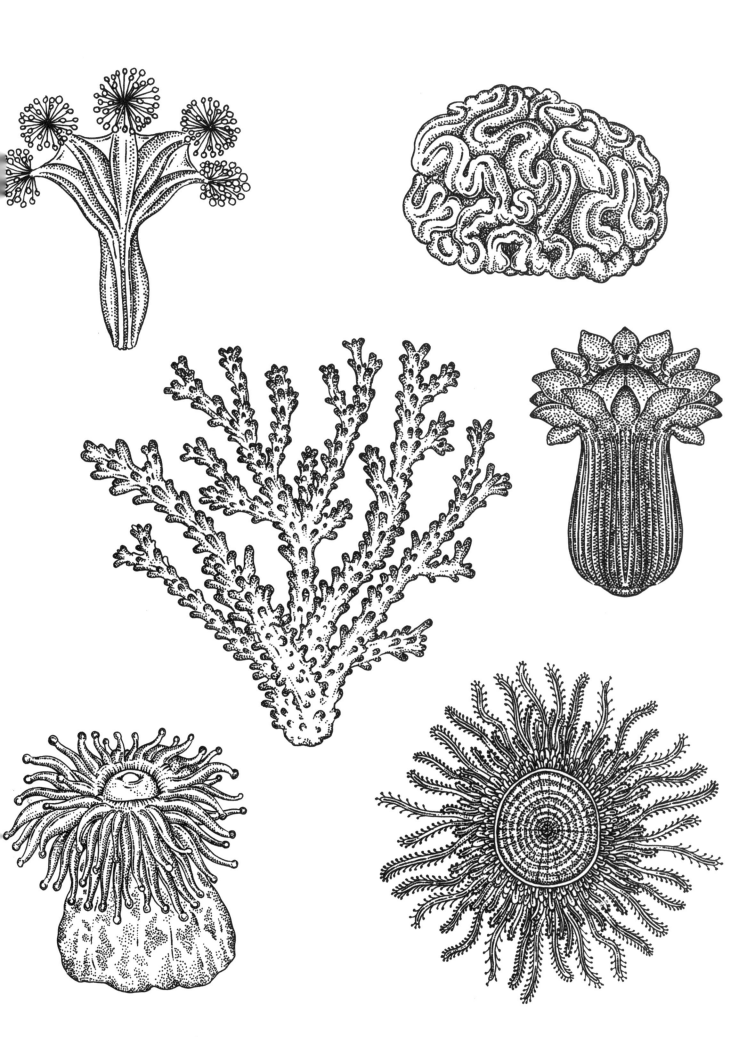

Hoofed Mammals

Hoofed mammals vary wildly, from the huge and powerful rhinoceros to the elegant gazelle. Despite differences in appearance, hoofed mammals all have toes strengthened by a thick, horny covering similar to toenails, which never stops growing, and is worn down by constant use. Many have horns or antlers made of bone protruding from their heads, which they use to defend themselves from predators. Some species, such as deer, will demonstrate their strength by locking horns with a rival, hoping to impress a female.

Squid

The slow-moving, alien-like long-armed squid *(right)* lives at depths of up to 2.4 kilometres. Although it looks alarming, it is only 12.5 centimetres long. The whip-lash squid *(left)* is even smaller, at only 10 centimetres long. Its long, whip-like tentacles are all covered in tiny, sticky suckers. Squid's large brains and advanced senses make them sociable creatures able to communicate with one another – they sometimes even shoal with fish for company.

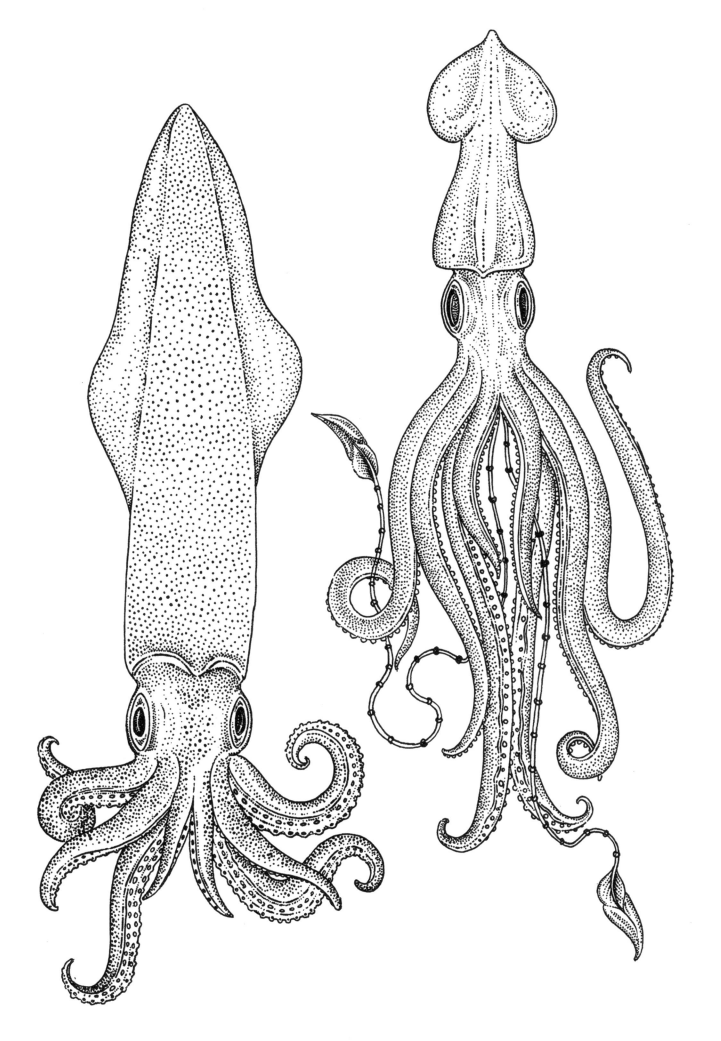

BIG PICTURE PRESS

First published in the UK in 2016 by Big Picture Press,
part of the Bonnier Publishing Group,
The Plaza, 535 King's Road, London, SW10 0SZ
www.bigpicturepress.net
www.bonnierpublishing.com

1 3 5 7 9 10 8 6 4 2
0516 002

ISBN 978-1-78370-612-9

This book was typeset in Gill Sans and Mrs Green
The illustrations were created with pen and ink and coloured digitally

Designed by Wendy Bartlet
Text by Jenny Broom
Edited by Ruth Symons

Printed in China